For David ~ M.H
For my family and friends ~ C.C

First published in Great Britain in 1996 by
Frances Lincoln Children's Books,
74-77 White Lion Street,
London N1 9PF
www.franceslincoln.com

First paperback edition 1997

The author and artist would like to thank Dr Wendy Kirk of the
Department of Geological Sciences, University College, London, and Dr Angela Milner
of the Department of Palaeontology, The Natural History Museum, London, for their help.

A catalogue record of this book is available from the British Library.

ISBN 978–0–7112–1076–9

Printed in China

The Pebble in my Pocket

A History of our Earth

MEREDITH HOOPER

Illustrated by CHRIS COADY

F

FRANCES LINCOLN
CHILDREN'S BOOKS

At the back of the book is a geological time line charting the main periods in earth's history, from around 4600 million years ago to the present day. Animals not named in the text are labelled on the time line.

Although the story of The Pebble in my Pocket traces the way a single pebble is formed, the animals illustrated come from various locations and were chosen as typical of the geological times in which they lived.

THE PEBBLE in my pocket is round and smooth and brown.
I found it on the ground.
Where did you come from, pebble?

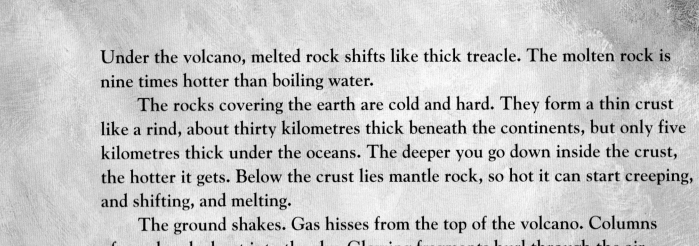

Under the volcano, melted rock shifts like thick treacle. The molten rock is nine times hotter than boiling water.

The rocks covering the earth are cold and hard. They form a thin crust like a rind, about thirty kilometres thick beneath the continents, but only five kilometres thick under the oceans. The deeper you go down inside the crust, the hotter it gets. Below the crust lies mantle rock, so hot it can start creeping, and shifting, and melting.

The ground shakes. Gas hisses from the top of the volcano. Columns of purple ash shoot into the sky. Glowing fragments hurl through the air. Then the lava comes, molten rock spilling red-hot down the volcano's sides, and flowing out over the land.

The lava cools. It hardens, forming a thick, wrinkled skin of new rock.

Everything is still. The seas swarm with living things. But nothing is living on this land.

It is 480 million years ago.

Slowly, very slowly, the surface of the earth begins rising.
The rock made from the lava begins to tilt up, slowly,
very slowly. All the rocks underneath go up. Everything
that happens to be on this piece of earth is rising. Huge
slabs of rock tilt, and twist. The land folds and buckles
and crumples.

Two great landmasses, like giant plates, are colliding,
pushing against each other, making mountains.

Every winter snow falls. Every summer the snow melts
and the sun shines on the rocks. Heat makes the rocks
expand. Cold makes them shrink. They expand and shrink,
expand and shrink. Then they crack.

Water seeps into cracks in the rocks. On cold nights
the water freezes. Clear crystals of ice push inside the cracks,
wedging pieces of rock slowly apart.

Rain falls on the mountains and runs down the rocks.
Little leafless plants grow in damp places, because now
some things are living on the land.

It is 395 million years ago.

In the middle of summer, in the middle of the night, an enormous slice of cliff splits away from a mountainside and crashes down, shattering into fragments. Pieces of rock rumble and bounce down the mountain like a river of stone.

Rain falls on the new jagged edges of the rock, and the hot sun heats it, and the frost cools it. The wind blows, every day. Tiny specks of sand blow against the corners and edges of the rock, nibbling at their sharpness. Slowly, slowly, the sharp edges begin to be smoothed.

Everything on the surface of the earth is slowly being eroded and broken down into smaller and smaller pieces. Boulders powder into streaks of mud. Cliffs crumble to grains of sand. The tops of mountains disintegrate into pebbles. It has always happened. It will always happen. It is happening now. All that is needed is time.
And the weather.

Worm-like creatures burrow in moss jungles and millipedes shelter under the rock.
It is 390 million years ago.

The rain pours down, loosening the earth. Mud and rocks slide off the mountainside into a river. The river rushes along, dragging silt, sand, gravel, boulders, stripping away the mountain's surface, layer by layer.

The river tumbles and rolls the rock, chipping edges, smoothing corners, rubbing it against other rocks. Gradually the rock becomes rounder, smaller. The river widens, flowing brown and slow.

The current nudges the rock past forests of ferns where spiders hide. It eases the rock through swamps where fish haul themselves out of the water and breathe the air.

The rock travels for thousands and thousands of years. When it reaches the sea it is a smooth, round, brown pebble.

It is 375 million years ago.

Boulders and rocks embedded deep in the soil of the mountain look like permanent residents. They aren't. They are just passing through, like everything else, all on the way to the bottom of the sea.

The river drops the pebble on to a beach filled with other pebbles. The waves of the sea wash them backwards and forwards, grinding them up and grinding them down, rattling and clinking the pebbles together: stripy pebbles, spotted pebbles, grey, brown and white pebbles. Each pebble has come from its own special rock. Each was made in its own time and place.

Shiny grains of sand settle between the pebbles. The sand fills the spaces like the mixture between pieces of fruit in a pudding.

Slowly the sea starts to flood the land. The sea covers the pebbles packed in their grains of sand. Gradually the sand hardens, forming a new layer of rock, a conglomerate 'pudding-stone' rock. The sea covers the cliffs, and drowns the mouth of the river, and washes into the forests.

It is 340 million years ago.

Creatures swarm and slither in the warm sea.
The tiny bodies of dead sea creatures drift down
on to the seabed, layer upon layer. Fine mud
drifts down, and sand. As each layer presses down,
the layers beneath slowly harden and the particles
cement together to form more rock, layers of
sedimentary rock under the sea.

A meat-eating dinosaur attacks a plant-eating dinosaur. In the fight the pebble skids into a river. The pebble settles on to a sand bar, with dinosaur bones and driftwood, drowned moths and flowers, because now there are flowers in this land.

It is 65 million years ago.

The river flows in a new course, and the pebble lies buried
in the old river bed. The dinosaurs have long since died out.
Now, grass grows, and herds of long-legged animals graze
above the pebble. A furry, two-horned rodent pushes past
the pebble in its burrow.

It is 15 million years ago.

The wind blows colder and colder. Snow falls. Blizzards blot out the light. The snow packs down, layer on layer. Deep underneath the surface snow, the old snow turns into clear blue glacier ice.

The glacier starts shifting, moving slowly down hill, grinding forward, a monstrous river of ice scraping across the land, scouring out valleys, sculpting mountains. The glacier picks up and moves everything in its way. It picks up the pebble and freezes it deep in its icy blue depths.

The glacier grinds on for thousands and thousands of years, roaring and groaning as the ice slides and shifts. Its surface is split with shadowy crevasses.

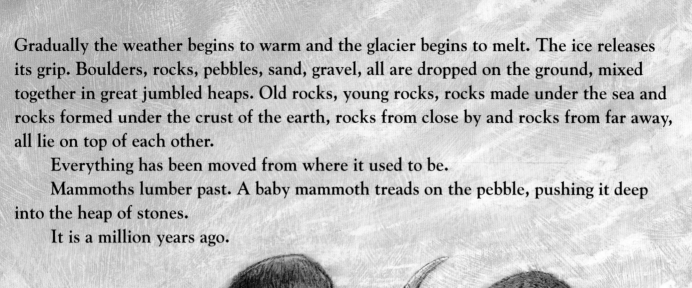

Gradually the weather begins to warm and the glacier begins to melt. The ice releases its grip. Boulders, rocks, pebbles, sand, gravel, all are dropped on the ground, mixed together in great jumbled heaps. Old rocks, young rocks, rocks made under the sea and rocks formed under the crust of the earth, rocks from close by and rocks from far away, all lie on top of each other.

Everything has been moved from where it used to be.

Mammoths lumber past. A baby mammoth treads on the pebble, pushing it deep into the heap of stones.

It is a million years ago.

Floods leave the pebble high on a river bank. People come to fish and hunt, and build shelters. They stand on the pebble and sleep on it and drop grease from half-cooked lumps of meat.

In the night a rat creeps in, sniffing for food. A boy picks up the pebble to throw at the rat. He misses. The pebble rolls under a bush and down a hole.

It is 200,000 years ago.

The cold comes back. People move away. Massive ice sheets cover the land, burying forests and meadows. When warmth returns, the melting ice drops the pebble in a lake. It sinks into the soft mud, while hippos wallow above in the warm water.

It is 125,000 years ago.

A new glacier gouges the pebble out of the bottom of the lake and pushes it, clasped in its clear blue depths, for thousands and thousands of years. Then the ice retreats, leaving the pebble on the slope of a valley.

Shaggy bison graze the long grass. New people come, hunting for food. Sabre-tooth tigers watch. They can hunt what they like.

It is 12,000 years ago.

The pebble hasn't moved much since the last ice age.

It has been kicked and trodden on, by animals and people. Cattle have grazed over it. Farmers have grown crops on it. A new road runs near it. Houses are built next to the road, and their foundations cover rocks and earth, pebbles and gravel.

But the houses miss the pebble. It lies, smooth and warm, in the sun.

The pebble in my pocket is round and smooth and brown. I found it on the ground.

My pebble has been on top of mountains and under the sea. It has been buried in ice and buried in rock. It has been covered in drying sand and tropical forest. It has been flung and dropped, frozen, soaked and baked, squeezed and squashed. It has been stood on and sheltered under and used. It has travelled huge distances, over immense periods of time.

My pebble is four hundred and eighty million years old. So far.
Keep travelling, pebble!

Every pebble in the world is different from every other pebble.
Every pebble has its own story. Pick up a pebble and you are holding
a little piece of the history of our planet.

When did it all happen?

The story of *The Pebble in my Pocket* begins with a lava flow from an erupting volcano, 480 million years ago. Nine-tenths of earth's history has already happened. Geological changes occur over staggeringly huge periods of time. They are caused by constant tiny events, difficult to see - the action of water, wind and sun, and the downward pull of gravity. They are everyday forces which happen every day. They have always happened, and they are happening right now.

Geologists divide the earth's history into various time periods. The chart on the right is a geological time line, from the beginnings of the earth, around 4600 million years ago, to the present day. Some of the animals that appear in this book are shown below.

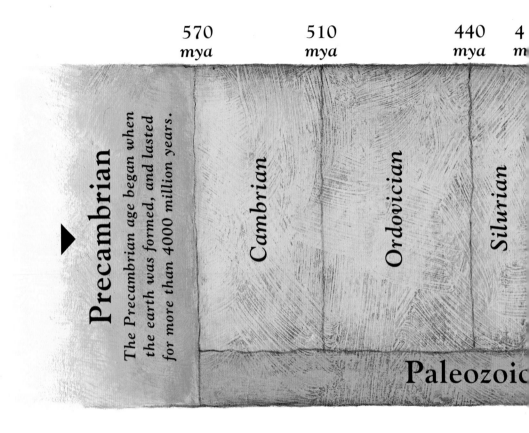

570 mya   510 mya   440 mya   4 m

Precambrian
The Precambrian age began when the earth was formed, and lasted for more than 4000 million years.

Cambrian

Ordovician

Silurian

Paleozoic

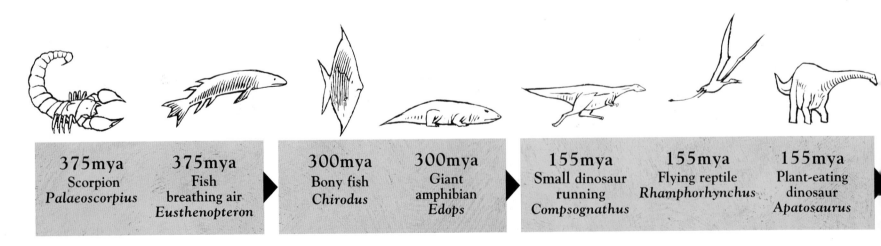

375mya
Scorpion
Palaeoscorpius

375mya
Fish breathing air
Eusthenopteron

300mya
Bony fish
Chirodus

300mya
Giant amphibian
Edops

155mya
Small dinosaur running
Compsognathus

155mya
Flying reptile
Rhamphorhynchus

155mya
Plant-eating dinosaur
Apatosaurus

These pictures are not drawn to scale.

mya= million years ago

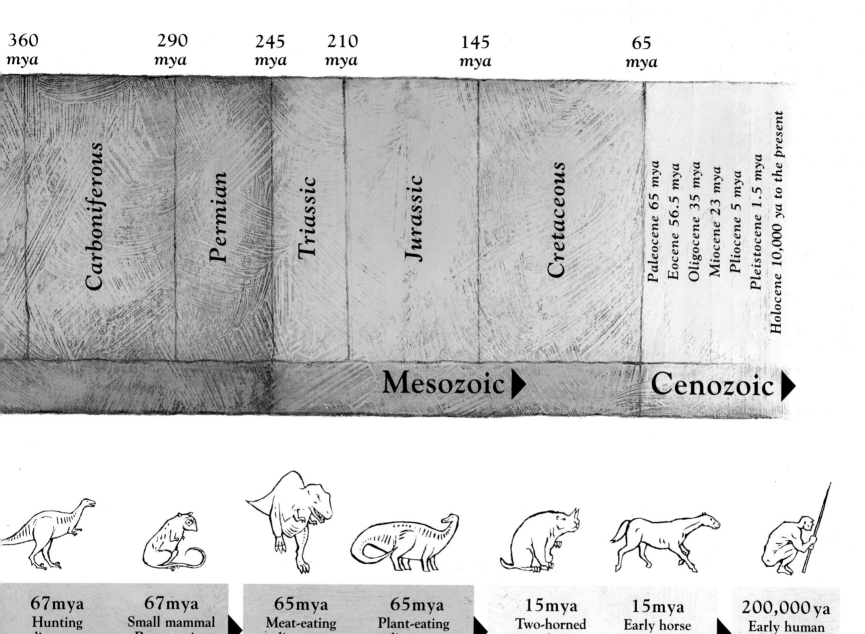

360 mya

290 mya

245 mya

210 mya

145 mya

65 mya

Carboniferous

Permian

Triassic

Jurassic

Cretaceous

Paleocene 65 mya
Eocene 56.5 mya
Oligocene 35 mya
Miocene 23 mya
Pliocene 5 mya
Pleistocene 1.5 mya
Holocene 10,000 ya to the present

Mesozoic ▶

Cenozoic ▶

67mya Hunting dinosaur *Dromaeosaurus*

67mya Small mammal *Purgatorius*

65mya Meat-eating dinosaur *Tyrannosaurus*

65mya Plant-eating dinosaur *Edmontosaurus*

15mya Two-horned rodent *Epigaulus*

15mya Early horse *Merychippus*

200,000ya Early human *Neanderthal*

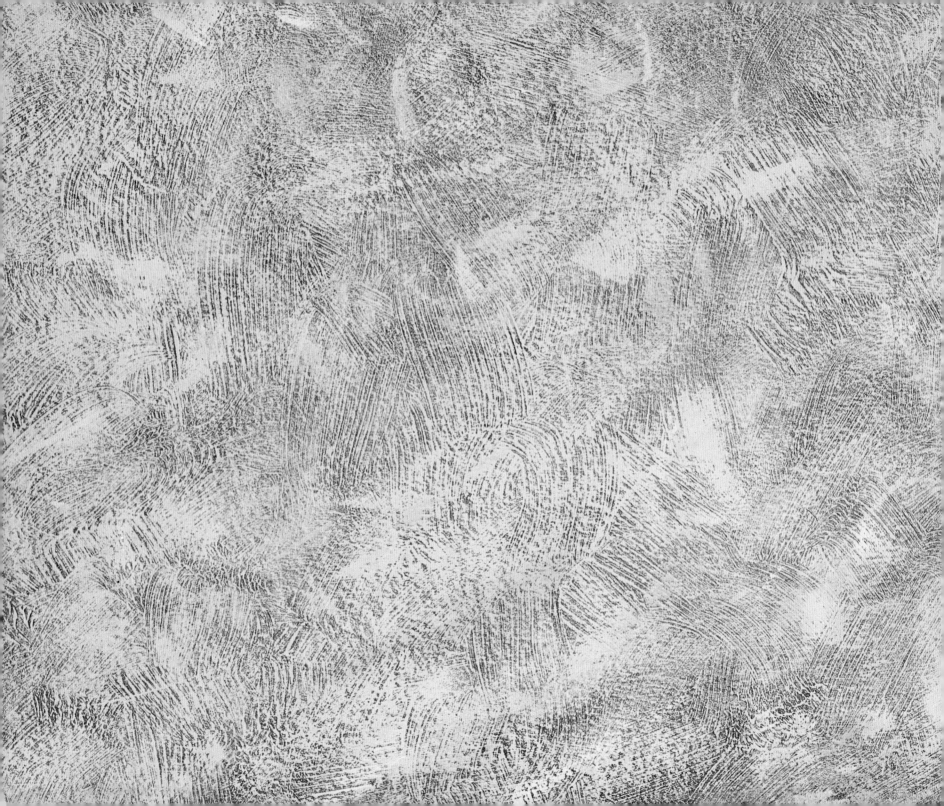

MORE PICTURE BOOKS BY MEREDITH HOOPER
FROM FRANCES LINCOLN

Ice Trap!

Shackleton's Incredible Expedition

Illustrated by M. P. Robertson

Sir Ernest Shackleton's ship *Endurance* has been crushed by ice! Shackleton and his 27 men were
attempting to cross Antarctica, but now they are stranded on an ice flow, hundreds of miles from land.
Undaunted by danger, they embark on a courageous journey back to civilization,
in one of the most remarkable true-life adventure stories ever!

The Drop In My Drink

Illustrated by Chris Coady

The intriguing story of a drop of water, from the beginnings of our
planet to the water cycle of today. Meredith Hooper takes us back thousands of years to see where
the Earth's water came from, and how life began in the oceans and later moved onto land.
She describes the water cycle, the relationship between water and living things and between water and erosion.
She also discusses important environmental issues and provides a fascinating collection of water facts.

Tom Crean's Rabbit

A True Story from Scott's Last Voyage

Illustrated by Bert Kitchen

It's very cold in Antarctica, and Tom the sailor is looking for a quiet, cosy place on the ship for his pet rabbit.
Based on diaries of men from Captain Scott's second expedition to the South Pole.

Frances Lincoln titles are available from all good bookshops.

Prices are correct at time of publication, but may be subject to change.